Where is Sid?

First published in 2008
by Wayland

Wayland
338 Euston Road
London NW1 3BH

Wayland Australia
Hachette Children's Books
Level 17/207 Kent Street
Sydney, NSW 2000

Series editor: Louise John
Cover design: Paul Cherrill
Design: D.R.ink
Consultant: Shirley Bickler

A CIP catalogue record for this book is available from the British Library.

ISBN 9780750251815 (hbk)

Printed in China

Wayland is a division of Hachette Children's Books,
an Hachette Livre UK Company

Where is Sid?

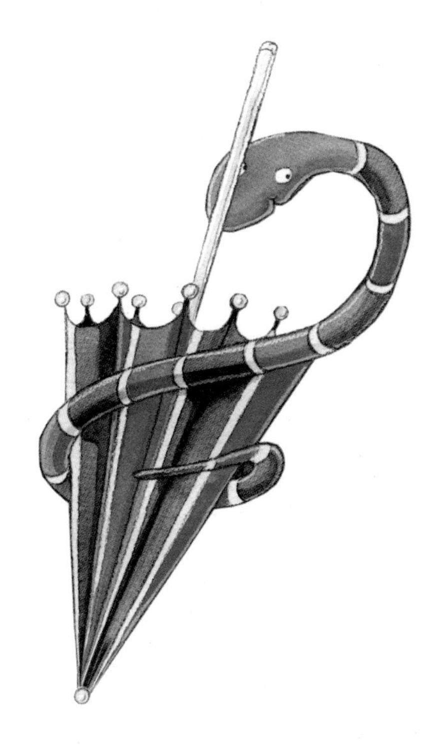

Written by Claire Llewellyn
Illustrated by Jacqueline East

WAYLAND

Pip got up on Sunday.
He looked for Sid, but
he wasn't in his tank.

Pip looked in the sitting room.

Sid wasn't there.

Pip looked outside, but
Sid wasn't in the garden.

"Where are you, Sid?" he said.

Pip went into the
garden shed.

He looked behind the tools,
but Sid wasn't hiding there.

Next, he looked in
Mum's car.

No luck. That snake was hard to find!

Mum was in the kitchen.
"Have you seen Sid?"
said Pip.

“No,” she said.
“He isn’t here.”

Next, Pip looked in the cupboard.

"Are you in there, Sid?" he asked.

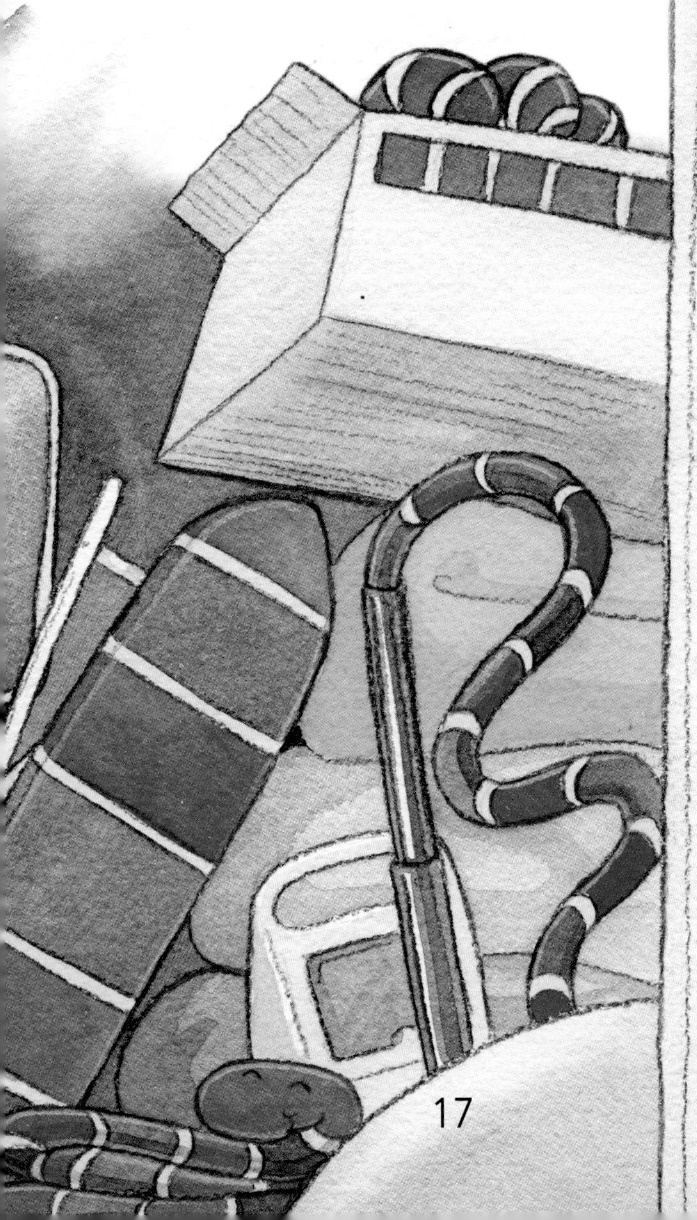

Then it was time for bed. Pip got undressed and he put on his pyjamas.

“Oh, Sid!” he said.
“Where are you?”

Pip went into the bathroom.
He brushed his teeth.

He was sad.

Then Pip got into bed...

...and there was Sid.

“Here you are at last!” said Pip.

START READING is a series of highly enjoyable books for beginner readers. They have been carefully graded to match the Book Bands widely used in schools. This enables readers to be sure they choose books that match their own reading ability.

The Bands are:

- Pink / Band 1
- Red / Band 2
- Yellow / Band 3
- Blue / Band 4
- Green / Band 5
- Orange / Band 6
- Turquoise / Band 7
- Purple / Band 8
- Gold / Band 9

START READING books can be read independently or shared with an adult. They promote the enjoyment of reading through satisfying stories supported by fun illustrations.

Claire Llewellyn has written many books for children. Some of them are about real things like animals or the Moon. Others are storybooks, like this one. Claire has two children of her own, but they are getting too big for stories like this. She hopes that you will enjoy reading her stories instead now!

Jacqueline East scratched her first drawing into her mum's sideboard when she was six! She has enjoyed drawing animals ever since and has a naughty dog called Scampi, who often appears in her books! When Jacqueline is not drawing, she likes to dance and play the guitar.